Bordaria
Difendere con Coraggio

D1310246

Scholastic Canada Ltd.
604 King Street West, Toronto, Ontario M5V 1E1, Canada

Scholastic Inc.
557 Broadway, New York, NY 10012, USA

Scholastic Australia Pty Limited
PO Box 579, Gosford, NSW 2250, Australia

Scholastic New Zealand Limited
Private Bag 94407, Botany, Manukau 2163, New Zealand

Scholastic Children's Books
Euston House, 24 Eversholt Street, London NW1 1DB, UK

PÖP & FÏZZ

Text, design and illustration copyright © Lemonfizz Media, 2010.
Cover illustration by Yohann Schepacz.
Internal illustrations by Lionel Portier, Melanie Matthews and James Hart.
First published by Pop & Fizz and Scholastic Australia in 2010.
Pop & Fizz is a partnership between Paddlepop Press and Lemonfizz Media.
www.paddlepoppress.com
This edition published under licence from Scholastic Australia Pty Limited.
on behalf of Lemonfizz Media.

First published by Scholastic Australia in 2010.
This edition published by Scholastic Canada Ltd., 2011.

Library and Archives Canada Cataloguing in Publication

Park, Mac

Terradon / Mac Park ; illustrations by Melanie Matthews, Lionel Portier

and James Hart.

(Boy vs beast. Battle of the worlds)

ISBN 978-1-4431-0748-8

I. Matthews, Melanie, 1986- II. Portier, Lionel

III. Hart, James, 1981- IV. Title. V. Series: Park, Mac.

Boy vs beast. Battle of the worlds.

PZ7.P2213Te 2011   j823'.92   C2010-907355-X

6 5 4 3 2 1   Printed in Canada 116   11 12 13 14 15

BOY VS BEAST

BATTLE OF THE WORLDS

TERRADON

Mac Park

POP & FIZZ

SCHOLASTIC

Prologue

Once, mega-beast and man shared one world. But it did not last. The beasts wanted to rule the world. They started battles against man. After many bad battles between beast and man, the world was split in two. Man was given Earth. Mega-beasts were given Beastium.

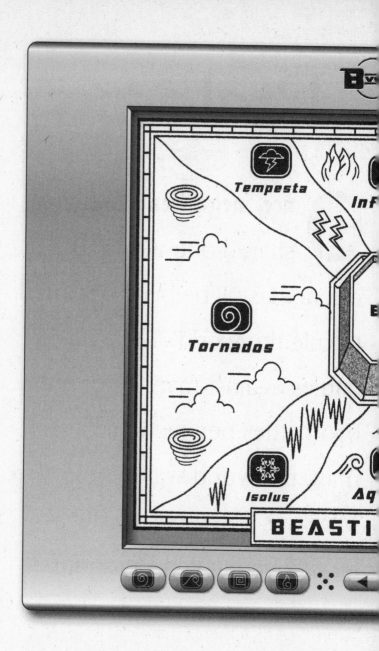

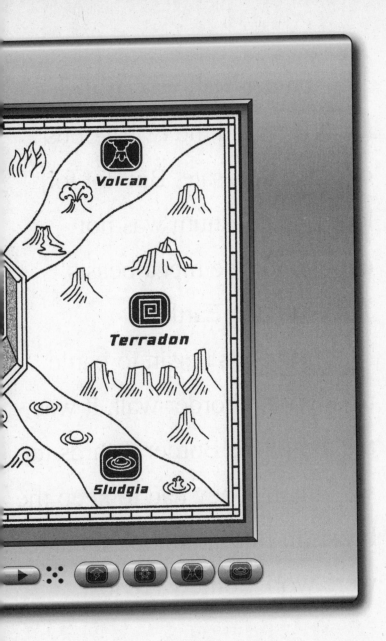

Volcan

Terradon

Sludgia

A border-wall was created. It closed the two worlds off. Man was safe. But not for long . . . Beastium was not enough for the mega-beasts. They wanted Earth.

The beasts began to battle through the border-wall. It was the job of the Border Guards to stop them. They had to keep the beasts in Beastium. Some battles were won. Some were lost.

Battles won by the beasts gave them more power. The beasts earned new battle attacks. Battles won by the Border Guards earned them upgrades. Their battle gear could do more.

Five boys now guard the border-wall. They are the Bordaria Border Guards. They are in training to become Border Masters like their dads.

The Bordaria Master Command

The Border Guards' dads and granddads are the Bordaria Master Command. The BMC helps the Border Guards during battle.

The Border Guards must learn. The safety of Earth depends on them.

The BMC rewards good Border Guard battling. Upgrades can be earned for sending beasts back into their lands. New battle gear can also be given to Border Guards who battle well.

If they do not battle well, the Border Guards will lose upgrades and points. Then they will not be given new and better gear.

Kai Masters is a Border Guard in training. His work is top secret. He must protect Earth. The BMC watches Kai closely. Kai must not fail.

Let the battles commence!

Chapter 1

Kai Masters was just like
any twelve-year-old boy.
But Kai was also a Beastium
Border Guard. Kai's dad and
granddad were once Border
Guards, too. They became
Border Masters. Now they
are part of the Bordaria
Master Command. The BMC.

It was their job to teach
Kai. And help him during
battles. It was Kai's job to
keep Earth safe from beasts.
Beasts who tried to break
through the border-wall.

Kai lived in the old
lighthouse on the hill.
The outside of it was very
old. The inside was built just
for Border Guards. It was
totally high-tech.

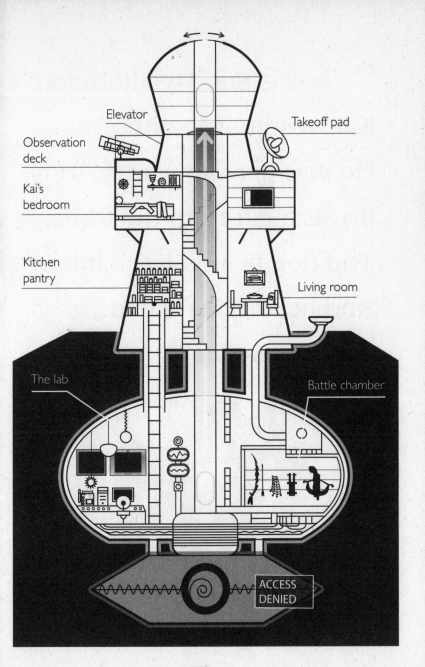

Observation deck

Elevator

Takeoff pad

Kai's bedroom

Kitchen pantry

Living room

The lab

Battle chamber

ACCESS DENIED

15

It was Sunday afternoon.

Kai was in his bedroom.

He was playing with his dog.

It was a gift from the BMC.

The dog helped Kai battle.

And he was his friend.

ROBOTIC CANINE BC3

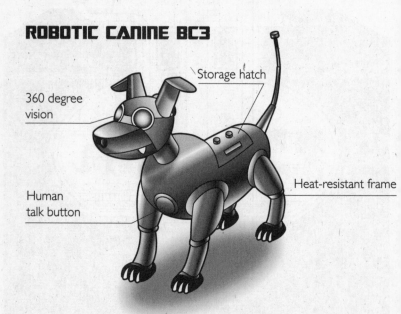

Storage hatch

360 degree
vision

Heat-resistant frame

Human
talk button

The dogbot could talk. And it could think. It was just like a person, really. Well, not quite. It did have a few computer bugs that Kai had to deal with.

The dog was known as BC3. Kai called him BC for short. BC could hear everything. And he could see behind himself. BC was a very smart dog.

Kai looked at the dog. His tail was wagging.

"You think there's trouble coming?" Kai asked.

BC always wagged his tail when there was trouble.

"You're meant to bark when there is trouble!"

"Dirt is falling," said BC.

Dirt falling, thought Kai. *What could he mean?*

Kai turned on the TV.

Kai had eight TVs to pick from. A news flash popped up on a screen. The news reader's voice filled the room.

"At 12:15 p.m. today a huge pile of rocks fell onto Bent Road. The rocks are so hot, they can't be moved."

All those rocks have blocked the road off, thought Kai. He took a closer look at the TV.

"Those rocks are melting the road! We'd better get over there, BC," said Kai. "Something's wrong. We need some of that rock."

Kai grabbed his orbix. It was a gift from his dad. It had a computer in it. The BMC used it to talk with their guards. It could do lots of things. It could even pick up super-hot rocks.

THE ORBIX

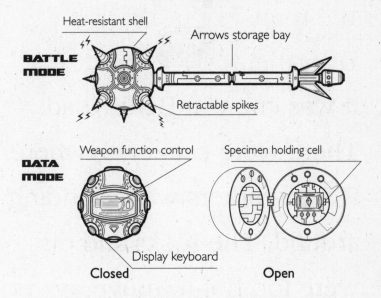

BATTLE MODE
Heat-resistant shell
Arrows storage bay
Retractable spikes

DATA MODE
Weapon function control
Specimen holding cell
Display keyboard
Closed   **Open**

Kai put BC in his
backpack. Then he jumped
on his bike. He rode to Bent
Road.

Chapter 2

It was crazy at Bent Road. There were cars everywhere. Road workers were standing around. The rocks and dirt were too hot to move.

Kai went over to the rocks. He took out his orb and keyed in

 Get sample

A metal arm shot out from the orb. It had a hand on the end of it. It picked up a small piece of rock. Then the arm and rock went back inside the orb. It was very fast and no one saw it. *This isn't just any rock,* thought Kai. *I need to get this to the lab fast. I think beasts have broken through the border-wall again.*

Kai raced back to the lighthouse. He went into the kitchen. The lab was hidden under it. Kai walked into the pantry. He pushed the secret button. It was under the bottom shelf.

The back wall of the pantry slid open. There was a ladder behind the wall. Kai went down the ladder and into his lab.

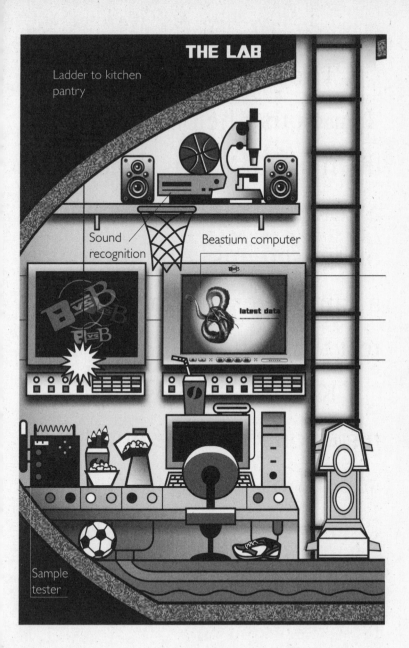

THE LAB

Ladder to kitchen pantry

Sound recognition

Beastium computer

latest data

Sample tester

The lab had lots of things. Things that helped Kai to learn about beasts. There was a computer. There were lots of big screens. And there was a sample tester. Kai used it to test things he found.

Kai turned the sample tester on. Then he put the super-hot rock in it.

He clicked the test button on the computer.

The screen flashed.

Two Beastium lands
popped up. *The rock land,*
thought Kai. *And the fire
land. It can only be one land.*

But which one? Hot rock. But rock mostly. Kai hit the rock land button. A beast I.D. card popped up.

BEAST
I.D.

TERRAMINISAUR
Small but tricky

Strength	★ ☆ ☆ ☆ ☆
Attack Power	★ ⯪ ☆ ☆ ☆
Speed	⯪ ☆ ☆ ☆ ☆

Then the computer
screen flashed again.

"So it's changed," said
Kai. "It's something new. It's
a big beast now. It's hard
to know what we will be
battling."

Chapter 3

"We'd better get ready for battle, BC," said Kai. He took out his Border Guard Card. He put it into the computer slot. Then there was a very loud noise.

CLUNK!
BANG!

Whiiiir! BANG!

Four big bricks in the
back wall moved. They left
a hole. Kai went through
the hole into the room.
The battle chamber had
three walls. They were filled
with things. Kai looked at
the third wall. It had a screen
over it. *I can't see this wall,*
thought Kai. *Even though I
won the water battle.*

And that's when Kai saw the TD5. It was on the middle wall. It looked so hot! "That's what we need, BC," said Kai. "We'll be able to get things from this wall for sure now." Kai went to take it. He heard the sound of a lock closing.

CLUNK! GRRRR **CLUNK!**

Then a computer voice said,

"Not yet!"

"We're still stuck with the first wall, BC," said Kai. "The BMC have the other walls locked." He went to the first wall. Kai looked at a bow. "This will do us, BC," said Kai.

"This thing can shoot into rocks. We can only take one other thing now." Kai looked at everything on the wall.

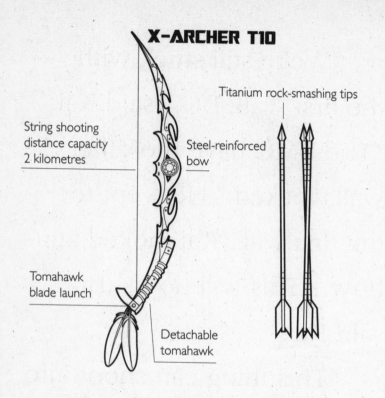

X-ARCHER T10

Titanium rock-smashing tips

String shooting
distance capacity
2 kilometres

Steel-reinforced
bow

Tomahawk
blade launch

Detachable
tomahawk

Then he chose the net.
"This net can catch all kinds
of things," said Kai. "And put
them to sleep!"

BEASTARI NET

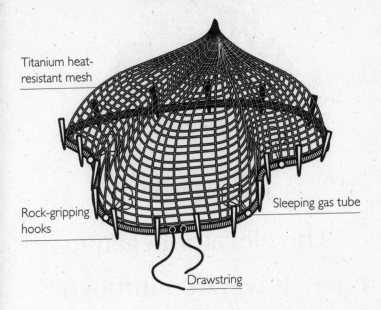

Titanium heat-resistant mesh

Rock-gripping hooks

Sleeping gas tube

Drawstring

Kai and BC went into the elevator. It took them to the takeoff pad. Kai took out his orb. He keyed in the code for the rock land.

The elevator began to move. It went up through the lighthouse. By the time he reached the top floor, Kai was in full battle gear.

The BMC has given my clothes Armour-All!

The same clothes. But now
they can take anything.
Even rocks won't hurt me,
thought Kai.

BC stood beside Kai, ready for battle. Kai's hoverboard was strapped to his feet. It had turbo rocket jets and could fly. "The hoverboard was excellent in our last battle, BC," said Kai. "We can't leave it behind."

THE HOVERBOARD

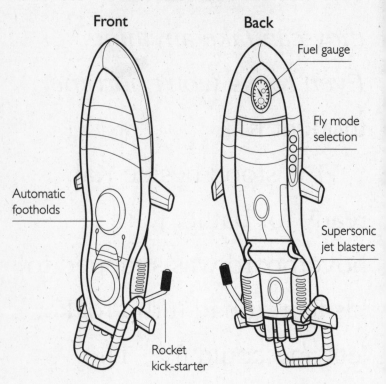

Front

Back

Fuel gauge

Fly mode
selection

Automatic
footholds

Supersonic
jet blasters

Rocket
kick-starter

Kai went to hit the light
button on the orb. But the
orb was flashing.

"My clothes are heatproof, too. We must have won that upgrade from our water battle," said Kai.

He hit the light button. The roof opened. The takeoff pad lit up.

The light shot up into the sky. In the blink of an eye they were gone.

Chapter 4

Kai and BC were in the rock land. It was hot and dry. There was rock and dirt everywhere Kai looked. But no beast. *Maybe I got it wrong,* thought Kai.

Kai kicked down on his hoverboard. He flew just above the ground.

Nothing but rock, thought Kai. *Where is this beast?*

Suddenly, BC shouted, "Noise attack!"

"I can't hear anything," said Kai. Then everything went dark. Kai heard a buzzing noise. And it was getting louder.

BZZZZZ BZZZZZ BZZZZZ

Kai turned and looked.
It was a group of flying rock
ants. It was headed straight
for them.

"Poison stingers!" warned
BC. *Great,* thought Kai,
just what we need. He flew
super-fast along the edge of
a big cliff. But the flying ants
were catching up fast.

Suddenly, the cliff edge
stopped. The drop was big.

Below was a huge, bowl-shaped rocky space.

The ants were very close. "It's now or never," said Kai. He jumped off the edge. The board flew through the air. It was just like he was flying.

Kai came down in the rocky space. He grabbed his orb. He took a photo of the flying ants.

Terra-toxic ants
No known cure
for poison

That's not good news, thought Kai.

Suddenly, the ants came down at them.

Kai took his net from his belt. He threw the net wide. It opened up.

The net caught all the ants in one go.

Kai pulled on the net's rope. It closed like a bag. Kai took out his orb and clicked

Net sleeping gas

A smelly gas came out from the net's tubes. It went all over the ants. They went very still. "They'll sleep for days and days," said Kai.

Kai jumped off his board. He picked up his net. As he did, he saw something stuck in the ground. "Get it, BC," said Kai.

BC's robot legs dug hard and fast. "It's an old arrowhead," said Kai. He put it in his pocket.

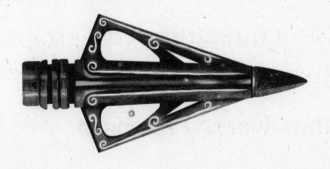

Chapter 5

Suddenly, BC said, "Hissing poison."

"It can't be the ants," said Kai. "They're all asleep."

Kai turned around quickly. Right in front of him was a three-headed Terra-rattlesnake. Its three sets of fangs were very sharp.

Kai threw his orb like a spinning ball. Blades flew out from each of its spikes. They flew through the snake's three heads.

Then the blades went back inside the orb. The orb flew back to Kai.

The heads fell to the ground. Kai turned to walk away when he heard

HISSS HISSS HISSS

The snake was still alive! And it was growing bodies and heads. Suddenly there were four snakes and twelve heads!

Kai threw the orb again. Twelve heads flew to the ground.

Then twelve snakes and thirty-six heads rose up from the dirt. The snakes moved up on them.

They were trapped. Kai's orb flashed. "Good," said Kai. "The orb blades have taken bits of the snake to test."

Terra-rattlesnake
Tomahawk + Feather
=
Feather Combo

What? thought Kai.

Combo? It sounds like a burger meal with fries.

Just then one of the three-headed snakes slid itself around Kai's leg.

Kai grabbed his bow.
He took the tomahawk off
the end of the bow. That was
when he saw the feathers.
What will these do? *It's time
for us to find out*, thought
Kai.

Kai pulled off a feather.
He pushed the tomahawk
blade through the feather.

Some blue stuff came out
of the feather's cut.

Kai threw the tomahawk. It hit the very first snake-head. Its three mouths dripped with blue stuff. Then it went away. All the other snakes went away with it.

"Why did they all go away?" asked BC.

"They were all part of the one snake," said Kai.

Chapter 6

Kai and BC sat down on the hard ground. "That was too close," said Kai.

Kai got back on his hoverboard. "This stays on my feet from now on," he said to BC. Kai bent to pick up BC. The dog wagged its tail again.

"Not more trouble, BC," said Kai.

"Shakes," said BC.

Then Kai felt it.
The ground shook.

BOOM!

RUMMMBLE!

BOOM!

Then it began to **CRAACCCCK**.

Kai grabbed BC. He hovered off the ground just in time.

The ground split into a big crack! The beast came out of the crack in the ground. It was no longer the beast that Kai knew. *It's the new beast,* thought Kai.

"We must beat it, BC," said Kai. "If we don't, it will be bigger and stronger than ever."

Kai took a quick photo of the beast with his orb.

The screen flashed.

TERRAMEGASAUR
Beware the pulver-slam

Kai grabbed his bow.

He fired two arrows at the beast. The arrows bounced straight off. The beast stomped its foot.

CRUMBLE!
CRAACCCCK!

The earth cracked open. Rocks began to fall from the cliffs. Kai and BC hovered against the rock wall. A great crack in the earth stood between boy and beast.

beast had buried them in a hole.
turned on his goggles to X-ray.

It's quiet. Maybe it thinks it's won and has left?

No. It's getting ready for its final move.

The beast lifted its tail. Once it hit the ground Kai, and BC would be finished.

Digging super fast.

Me too. We have to get out before its tail hits the ground.

The beast moved closer. Each step made the earth crack open more.

The earth opened up. Kai and BC fell down into the crack.

My arrows en't even slowing it down.

CRRRAACKK!

It's going to pulver-slam us with its tail again!

Oh no! It can't beat us. We can't . . .

e beast did one more pulver-slam. Rocks lled the crack. They buried Kai and BC. e beast had won.

GRRRREHHEHH HEH HEH HEHHHRR. . .

Chapter 7

Kai and BC were under the rocks. "Can you move, BC?" asked Kai.

"Yes," said the dog.

"I'm stuck," said Kai. "I can see the beast with my X-ray apps on my visor. It's going away. We need to get out."

BC started digging with his robotic legs. Just then Kai's orb beeped. BC pulled the orb from Kai's pocket with his teeth.

BC dropped the orb next to Kai's hands. Kai read the screen.

Use Ancient
Arrow Head
with X-Archer

"You have to get me out of here," Kai said to BC. "We can beat this beast."

The BMC had given Kai an idea.

"I'll work the hoverboard," said BC. The board was still on Kai's feet. It was pointing upward.

BC jumped onto Kai's legs. He used his robotic tail to kick-start the board.

The hoverboard's jets fired.

whiiiir whhiiiir

They hovered sideways. Then they pushed out from under the rocks. Kai slowly stood up. He took out the ancient arrowhead.

Kai took out an arrow. He took its arrowhead off. He put the old arrowhead on. It started to glow.

"This is our only hope," said Kai.

He flew up over the ground. The beast heard them. It slowly turned. Kai put the arrow in the bow. He pulled it back, ready to shoot.

The beast went up on its back legs. The beast's arms opened fire. Burning rocks flew straight at them.

Kai let his arrow go.
It flew through the air.
The arrow tip glowed. It hit
the beast. A terrible noise
filled the rock land.

FEEEEER
AAAAAARH
FEEER

Kai and BC watched as
the beast caught fire.

Then there was a huge blast.

KABOOM!

The beast smashed open. Rocks shot out all over the place.

Suddenly, the beast hit the ground. It turned into a pile of dust and dirt. It was no more. Kai had won.

Kai and BC had done the job they had come for.

Earth would be safe.

Chapter 8

Kai was just about to leave
when his orb flashed.
A small photo of the bow
came up on the screen.
Kai clicked on the photo.

"My bow has won
upgrades, BC!" said Kai.

"No upgrades for me?"
asked BC.

"Maybe," said Kai. "We don't always find out now. Sometimes we find out on our next battle. Come on. Time to go home." Kai took out his orb and he keyed in:

A bright white light shot down from the sky.

It grabbed Kai and BC.

It shot back up into the sky.

It took Kai and BC with it.

In the blink of an eye, they were gone.

TERRAMEGASAUR

This beast must pull itself together

Battle Plays	★ ☆ ☆ ☆ ☆
New Attacks	★ ☆ ☆ ☆ ☆
Energy	★ ⯪ ☆ ☆ ☆

Kai Masters

Kai rocks this battle

Battle Plays ★★★ ★★

Upgrades ★★ ★★★

Bonus Items ★ ★★★★

BATTLE OF THE WORLDS
Have you read them all?